CHILDREN'S THRIFT CLASSICS

The Wizard of Oz

L. FRANK BAUM

Adapted by Bob Blaisdell
Illustrated by W. W. Denslow

DOVER PUBLICATIONS, INC.
New York

DOVER CHILDREN'S THRIFT CLASSICS
EDITOR OF THIS VOLUME: CANDACE WARD

Copyright

Copyright © 1995 by Dover Publications, Inc.
All rights reserved under Pan American and International Copyright Conventions.

Published in Canada by General Publishing Company, Ltd., 30 Lesmill Road, Don Mills, Toronto, Ontario.
Published in the United Kingdom by Constable and Company, Ltd., 3 The Lanchesters, 162–164 Fulham Palace Road, London W6 9ER.

Bibliographical Note

This Dover edition, first published in 1995, is a new abridgment of *The Wonderful Wizard of Oz* (first publication: George M. Hill Company, Chicago, 1900). The three full-page illustrations have been adapted by Thea Kliros from the original drawings by W. W. Denslow; the 35 vignette illustrations by W. W. Denslow are taken from the first edition and are here reproduced in black-and-white. The introductory Note has been specially prepared for this edition.

Library of Congress Cataloging-in-Publication Data

Baum, L. Frank (Lyman Frank), 1856–1919.
    The Wizard of Oz / L. Frank Baum ; abridged by Bob Blaisdell; [originally] illustrated by W. W. Denslow [adapted by Thea Kliros].
        p.   cm. — (Dover children's thrift classics)
    Summary: After a cyclone transports her to the land of Oz, Dorothy must seek out the great wizard in order to return to Kansas.
    ISBN 0-486-28585-5 (pbk.)
    [1. Fantasy.]   I. Blaisdell, Robert.   II. Denslow, W. W. (William Wallace), 1856–1915, ill.   III. Kliros, Thea, ill.   IV. Title.   V. Series.
PZ7.B327Wi   1995
[Fic]—dc20   95-9772
                                                                                    CIP
                                                                                     AC

Manufactured in the United States of America
Dover Publications, Inc., 31 East 2nd Street, Mineola, N.Y. 11501

Note

First published in 1900, *The Wonderful Wizard of Oz* was an immediate success. Its author, L[yman] Frank Baum, had tried his hand at many things before writing children's literature—newspaper reporter, stage manager, actor and traveling salesman. But today Baum is best remembered for his series of fantastic stories featuring Dorothy Gale, the Wizard of Oz and all the other characters inhabiting that magical realm.

Written "solely to pleasure children," Baum's first Oz book was, as he described it, "a modernized fairy tale, in which the wonderment and joy are retained and the heart-aches and nightmares are left out." Dorothy's journey to Oz and her search for a way to return to Kansas have a drama all their own—but there is never any doubt that she won't get back home. Instead, we can revel in her adventures with the Scarecrow, the Tin Woodman, Toto and the Cowardly Lion, and enjoy her defeat of the Wicked Witch of the West and her friendship with the Wizard.

Bob Blaisdell's new abridgment of Baum's tale, which retains the central plot elements of the original, is enhanced by 35 of the first edition's illustrations and three full-page adaptations of William Wallace Denslow's art.

Contents

1

The Cyclone and the Munchkins

DOROTHY LIVED on the great Kansas prairies, with Uncle Henry, who was a farmer, and Aunt Em, who was the farmer's wife. Their house was small. There were four walls, a floor and a roof. Uncle Henry and Aunt Em had a bed in one corner, and Dorothy had a little bed in another corner. There was no cellar—except a small hole called a cyclone cellar, where the family could go in case one of those great whirlwinds arose. It was reached by a trap-door in the middle of the floor.

When Dorothy stood in the doorway and looked around, she could see nothing but the great gray prairie on every side. Not a tree nor a house broke the broad sweep of flat country that reached the edge of the sky in all directions. The sun had baked the plowed land into a gray mass, with little cracks running through it. Even the grass was not green, for the sun had burned the tops of the long blades until they were the same gray color to be seen everywhere. Once the house had been painted, but the sun blis-

1

tered the paint and the rains washed it away, and now the house was as dull and gray as everything else.

When Aunt Em came there to live she was a young, pretty wife. The sun and wind had changed her, too. She was thin and gaunt, and never smiled, now. When Dorothy, who was an orphan, first came to her, Aunt Em had wondered that Dorothy could find anything to laugh at.

Uncle Henry never laughed. He was gray also, from his long beard to his boots, and he rarely spoke.

It was Toto that made Dorothy laugh, and saved her from growing as gray as her other surroundings. Toto was not gray; he was a little black dog, with long hair and small black eyes. Toto played all day long, and Dorothy played with him, and loved him dearly.

Today, however, they were not playing. Uncle Henry looked anxiously at the sky, which was even grayer than usual. Dorothy stood in the door with Toto in her arms, and looked at the sky too. Aunt Em was washing the dishes.

From the far north they heard a low wail of wind, and Uncle Henry and Dorothy could see where the long grass bowed in waves before the coming storm. There now came a sharp whistling in the air from the south, and they saw ripples in the grass coming from that direction also.

"There's a cyclone coming, Em," Uncle Henry called to his wife; "I'll go look after the stock."

"Quick, Dorothy!" Aunt Em screamed; "run for the cellar!"

Toto jumped out of Dorothy's arms and hid under the bed, and the girl started to get him. Aunt Em threw open the trap-door in the floor and climbed down the ladder. Dorothy caught Toto at last, and started to follow her aunt. When she was half way across the room there came a great shriek from the wind, and the house shook so hard that she lost her footing.

A strange thing then happened.

The house whirled around two or three times and rose slowly through the air. Dorothy felt as if she were going up in a balloon. The great pressure of the wind on every side of the house raised it up higher and higher, until it was at the very top of the cyclone; and there it remained and was carried miles and miles away as easily as you could carry a feather.

Hour after hour passed away. In spite of the swaying of the house and the wailing of the wind, Dorothy soon closed her eyes and fell fast asleep.

She was awakened by a shock. Dorothy sat up and noticed that the house was not moving; bright sunshine came in at the window. She sprang from her bed and with Toto at her heels ran and opened the door.

The cyclone had set the house down very gently—for a cyclone—in the midst of a country of marvelous beauty. There were lovely patches of green meadow, with trees bearing luscious fruits. Banks of gorgeous flowers were on every hand, and birds with brilliant plumage sang and fluttered in the trees. A little way off was a small brook.

While she stood looking at the strange and beautiful sights, she noticed coming toward her a group of the oddest people she had ever seen. They seemed about as tall as Dorothy, who was a well-grown child for her age, although they were, so far as looks go, many years older.

Three were men and one a woman, and all wore round hats that rose to a small point above their heads, with little bells around the brims. The hats of the men were blue; the little woman's hat was white, and she wore a white gown; over it were sprinkled little stars.

When these people drew near the house where Dorothy was standing in the doorway, they paused and whispered among themselves, as if afraid. But the little old woman walked up to Dorothy, made a low bow, and said, "You are welcome, noble Sorceress, to the land of the Munchkins. We are so grateful to you for having killed the Wicked Witch of the East, and for setting our people free from bondage."

What could the little woman possibly mean by calling Dorothy a sorceress, and saying she had killed the Wicked Witch of the East?

"You are very kind," said Dorothy, "but there must be some mistake. I have not killed anything."

"Your house did, anyway," replied the little old woman; "and that is the same thing. See!" she said, pointing to the corner of the house; "there are her two shoes, sticking out from under a block of wood."

Dorothy looked, and gave a little cry of fright. Two feet were, indeed, sticking out, shod in silver shoes with pointed toes.

"The Wicked Witch of the East," said the little woman, "has held all the Munchkins in bondage for many years, making them slave for her night and day.

Now they are all set free, and are grateful to you for the favor."

"Who are the Munchkins?" asked Dorothy.

"They are the people who live in this land of the East. I am their friend, although I live in the land of the North. I am the Witch of the North."

"Are you a real witch?" asked Dorothy.

"Yes," answered the woman. "But I am a good Witch, and people love me. I am not as powerful as the Wicked Witch was who ruled here, or I should have set the people free myself."

"But I thought all witches were wicked," said the girl.

"Oh, no. There were only four witches in all the Land of Oz, and two of them, those who live in the North and South, are good witches. Those who lived in the East and the West were, indeed, Wicked Witches; but now that you have killed one of them, there is but one Wicked Witch in all the Land of Oz— the one who lives in the West."

"But," said Dorothy, "Aunt Em, who lives in Kansas, where I come from, has told me that the witches were all dead."

The Witch of the North seemed to think for a time, then said, "I do not know where Kansas is. But tell me, is it a civilized country?"

"Oh, yes," replied Dorothy.

"Then that accounts for it. In the civilized countries there are no witches left; nor wizards, nor sorceresses. But, you see, the Land of Oz has never been civilized, for we are cut off from the rest of the world."

"Who are the Wizards?" asked Dorothy.

"Oz himself is the Great Wizard," answered the Witch. "He is more powerful than all the rest of us together. He lives in the City of Emeralds."

The Munchkins, who had been standing silently by, gave a loud shout.

The little old woman turned to look. The feet of the dead Witch had disappeared and nothing was left but the silver shoes.

"She was so old," explained the Witch of the North, "that she dried up in the sun. But the silver shoes are yours." She reached down and picked up the shoes, and after shaking the dust out of them handed them to Dorothy.

"There is some charm connected with them," said one of the Munchkins, "but what it is we never knew."

Dorothy set the shoes down in the house, and then said, "I am anxious to get back to my Aunt and Uncle. Can you help me find my way?"

They explained to her that there were deserts surrounding every direction around Oz. "I'm afraid, my dear," said the old lady, "you will have to live with us."

Dorothy began to sob, for she felt lonely among all these strange people. The little old woman took off her cap and balanced the point on the end of her nose, while she counted "one, two, three." At once the cap changed to a blackboard, on which was written in big, white chalk marks: "LET DOROTHY GO TO THE CITY OF EMERALDS."

"You must go to the City of Emeralds, Dorothy," said the woman. "Perhaps Oz will help you."

"Is he a good man?" asked the girl.

"He is a good wizard. Whether he is a man or not I cannot tell, for I have never seen him."

"How can I get there?" asked Dorothy.

"You must walk. It is a long journey, through a country that is sometimes pleasant and sometimes terrible. However, I will use all the magic arts I know of to keep you from harm. I will give you my kiss, and no one will dare injure a person who has been kissed by the Witch of the North."

When her lips touched the girl's forehead they left a round, shining mark.

"The road to the City of Emeralds is paved with
yellow brick," said the Witch; "so you cannot miss it.
When you get to Oz, tell your story and ask him to
help you. Goodbye, my dear."

The Witch gave Dorothy a friendly nod, whirled
around on her left heel three times, and disappeared,
much to the surprise of Toto, who barked after her
loudly enough when she had gone, because he had
been afraid even to growl while she stood by.

Dorothy began to feel hungry. She went to the
cupboard and cut herself some bread, which she
spread with butter. She gave some to Toto, and carried a pail down to the little brook and filled it with
water. Then after a good drink of the cool water for
herself and then Toto, she set about making ready for
the journey.

She dressed herself in her clean gingham dress,
with checks of white and blue, and tied a pink
sunbonnet on her head. She took a little basket and
filled it with bread. Then she looked down at her feet
and noticed how old and worn her shoes were.

She remembered the silver shoes that had belonged
to the Witch of the East and tried them on. They fitted
her as well as if they had been made for her.

"They would be just the thing to take a long walk
in," she said to Toto.

And so, with Toto trotting along behind her, she
started on her journey.

There were neat fences at the sides of the road,
painted blue, and beyond them were fields of grain

and vegetables. Evidently the Munchkins were good farmers and able to raise large crops. The blue houses of the Munchkins were round, with a big dome for a roof.

Towards evening, when Dorothy was tired, she came to a large house. On the green lawn before it many men and women were dancing. The people greeted Dorothy and invited her to supper and to pass the night with them.

Dorothy ate a hearty supper and was waited upon by a rich Munchkin, whose name was Boq. When Boq saw her silver shoes he said, "You must be a great sorceress. You wear silver shoes and have killed the Wicked Witch. You have white in your frock, and only witches and sorceresses wear white."

"My dress is blue and white checked," said Dorothy.

"It is kind of you to wear that," said Boq. "Blue is the color of the Munchkins, and white is the witch color; so we know you are a friendly witch."

The next morning, Dorothy asked, "How far is it to the Emerald City?"

"I do not know," answered Boq. "But it will take you many days. The country here is rich and pleasant, but you must pass through rough and dangerous places before you reach the end of your journey."

2

The Scarecrow, the Tin Woodman
and the Cowardly Lion

S HE TOLD her friends goodbye, and again started along the road of yellow brick. When she had gone several miles she thought she would stop to rest, and so climbed to the top of the fence beside the road and sat down. There was a great cornfield beyond the fence, and not far away she saw a Scarecrow, placed high on a pole to keep the birds from the ripe corn.

The Scarecrow's head was a small sack stuffed with straw, with eyes, nose and mouth painted on it to represent a face. An old, pointed blue hat was perched on this head, and the rest of the figure was a blue suit of clothes which had also been stuffed with straw. On the feet were some old boots.

While Dorothy was looking into the odd, painted face of the Scarecrow, she was surprised to see one of the eyes wink at her. She thought she must have been mistaken, at first, for none of the scarecrows in Kansas ever wink; but presently the figure nodded its head to her. Then she climbed down from the fence and walked up to it, while Toto ran around the pole and barked.

"Good day," said the Scarecrow.

"Did you speak?" asked the girl.

"Certainly," answered the Scarecrow. "How do you do?"

"I'm pretty well, thank you," replied Dorothy; "how do you do?"

"I'm not feeling well," said the Scarecrow, "for it is very boring being perched up here night and day to scare away crows."

"Can't you get down?" asked Dorothy.

"No, for this pole is stuck up my back. If you will please take away the pole I shall be greatly obliged to you."

Dorothy reached up both arms and lifted the figure off the pole; for, being stuffed with straw, it was quite light.

"Thank you very much," said the Scarecrow, when he had been set down on the ground. "Who are you? And where are you going?"

"My name is Dorothy, and I am going to the Emerald City, to ask the great Oz to send me back to Kansas."

"Where is the Emerald City?" he asked. "And who is Oz? I don't know anything. You see, I am stuffed, so I have no brains at all. Do you think if I go to the Emerald City with you, that the great Oz would give me some brains?"

"I cannot tell," she answered. "But you may come with me, if you like."

"Thank you," he said.

They walked back to the road and started along the path of yellow brick for the Emerald City.

Toto did not like this addition to the party, at first. He often growled at the Scarecrow.

"Don't mind Toto," said Dorothy, to her new friend; "he never bites."

"Oh, I'm not afraid," said the Scarecrow, "he can't hurt the straw. I'll tell you a secret; there is only one thing in the world I am afraid of. A lighted match."

After a few hours the road began to be rough. There were fewer houses and fewer fruit trees. At noon they sat down by the roadside and Dorothy opened her basket and got out some bread. She offered a piece to the Scarecrow, but he refused.

"I am never hungry," he said; "and it is a lucky thing I am not. For my mouth is only painted, and if I should cut a hole in it so I could eat, the straw I am stuffed with would come out, and that would spoil the shape of my head."

Dorothy saw that this was true, so she went on eating her bread.

The Scarecrow asked her about herself, and she told him all about Kansas, and how gray everything was there.

The Scarecrow listened and then said, "I cannot understand why you should wish to leave this beautiful country and go back to the dry, gray place you call Kansas."

"That is because you have no brains," answered the girl. "No matter how dreary and gray our homes are, we people of flesh and blood would rather live there than in any other country, be it ever so beautiful. There is no place like home."

The Scarecrow sighed. "Of course I cannot understand it," he said. "If your heads were stuffed with straw, like mine, you would probably all live in the beautiful places, and then Kansas would have no people at all. It is fortunate for Kansas that you have brains."

Towards evening they came to a great forest, where the trees grew so big and close together that their branches met over the road of yellow brick.

"I see a little cottage at the right of us," said the Scarecrow, "built of logs and branches. Shall we go there?"

"Yes, indeed," said the child. "I am all tired out."

So the Scarecrow led her through the trees until
they reached the cottage, and Dorothy entered and
found a bed of dried leaves in one corner. She lay
down at once, and with Toto beside her soon fell into
a sound sleep. The Scarecrow, who was never tired,
stood up in another corner and waited patiently until
morning came.

When Dorothy awoke the sun was shining through
the trees. There was the Scarecrow still standing in
the corner, waiting for her.

When she had finished her breakfast of bread and
water, and was about to go back to the road of yellow
brick, she heard a deep groan near by.

She and the Scarecrow turned and walked through
the forest a few steps. One of the big trees had been
partly chopped through, and standing beside it, with
an uplifted axe in his hands, was a man made

entirely of tin. His head and arms and legs were jointed upon his body, but he stood perfectly motionless, as if he could not stir at all.

"Did you groan?" asked Dorothy.

"Yes," answered the tin man; "I did. I've been groaning for more than a year, and no one has ever heard me before or come to help me."

"What can I do for you?" she asked.

"Get an oil-can and oil my joints," he answered. "They are rusted so badly that I cannot move them at all; if I am well-oiled I shall soon be all right again. You will find an oil-can on a shelf in my cottage."

Dorothy ran back to the cottage and found the oil-can, and then she returned.

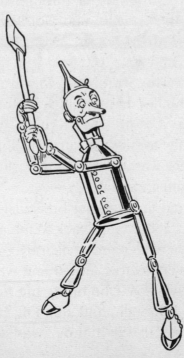

"Please, oil my neck, first," said the Tin Woodman. "Now oil the joints in my arms." The Tin Woodman gave a sigh and lowered his axe, which he leaned against the tree. "This is a great comfort," he said. "I have been holding that axe in the air ever since I rusted, and I'm glad to be able to put it down. Now, if you will oil the joints of my legs, I shall be all right once more."

He thanked them again and again; he seemed a very polite creature, and very grateful.

"I might have stood there always if you had not come along," he said; "so you have certainly saved my life. How did you happen to be here?"

"We are on our way to the Emerald City, to see the great Oz," she answered, "and we stopped at your cottage to pass the night."

"Why do you wish to see Oz?"

"I want him to send me back to Kansas; and the Scarecrow wants him to put a few brains into his head," she replied.

"Do you suppose Oz could give me a heart?"

"Why, I guess so," said Dorothy; "it would be as easy as to give the Scarecrow brains."

"True," the Tin Woodman said. "So, if you will allow me to join your party, I will also go to the Emerald City and ask Oz to help me."

"Come along," said the Scarecrow; and Dorothy added that she would be pleased to have his company.

Dorothy and her companions walked through the thick woods. The road was still paved with yellow brick, but these were much covered by dried branches and dead leaves from the trees.

"How long will it be," the child asked of the Tin Woodman, "before we are out of the forest?"

"I cannot tell," was the answer, "for I have never been to the Emerald City. I have heard it is a long journey through a dangerous country, but I am not afraid so long as I have my oil-can, and nothing can hurt the Scarecrow, while you bear upon your forehead the mark of the good Witch's kiss, and that will protect you from harm."

"But Toto!" said the girl; "what will protect him?"

"We must protect him ourselves," replied the Tin Woodman.

Just as he spoke there came from the forest a terrible roar, and the next moment a great Lion bounded into the road. With one blow of his paw he sent the Scarecrow spinning over and over to the edge of the road, and then he struck at the Tin Woodman with his sharp claws, and the Woodman fell over in the road and lay still.

Little Toto, now that he had an enemy to face, ran barking toward the Lion, and the great beast had opened his mouth to bite the dog, when Dorothy, fearing Toto would be killed, rushed forward and slapped the Lion upon his nose as hard as she could, while she cried out, "Don't you dare bite Toto! You ought to be ashamed of yourself, a big beast like you, to bite a poor little dog!"

"I didn't bite him," said the Lion, as he rubbed his nose with his paw.

"No, but you tried to," she said. "You are nothing but a big coward."

"I know it," said the Lion, hanging his head in shame; "I've always known it. But how can I help it?"

"I don't know, I'm sure. To think of your striking a stuffed man, like the poor Scarecrow!"

"Is he stuffed?" asked the Lion, as he watched her pick up the Scarecrow and pat him into shape again.

"Of course he's stuffed," replied Dorothy.

"Is the other one stuffed, also?" asked the Lion.

"No," said Dorothy, "he's made of tin." And she helped the Woodman up again.

"What is that little animal you are so tender of?"

"He is my dog, Toto," answered Dorothy.

"Is he made of tin, or stuffed?" asked the Lion.

"Neither. He's a—a—a meat dog," said the girl.

"Oh. He seems remarkably small, now that I look at him. No one would think of biting such a little thing except a coward like me," said the Lion.

"What makes you a coward?" asked Dorothy, looking at the great beast in wonder, for he was as big as a small horse.

"I suppose I was born that way," said the Lion. "All

the other animals in the forest naturally expect me to be brave. But if the elephants and the tigers and the bears had ever tried to fight me, I should have run myself—I'm such a coward; but just as soon as they hear me roar they all try to get away from me, and of course I let them go."

"But that isn't right. The King of Beasts shouldn't be a coward," said the Scarecrow.

"I know it," returned the Lion, wiping a tear from his eye with the tip of his tail.

"I am going to the great Oz to ask him to give me some brains," said the Scarecrow, "for my head is stuffed with straw."

"And I am going to ask him to give me a heart," said the Woodman.

"And I am going to ask him to send Toto and me back to Kansas," added Dorothy.

"Do you think Oz could give me courage?" asked the Cowardly Lion.

"Just as easily as he could give me brains," said the Scarecrow.

"Or give me a heart," said the Tin Woodman.

"Or send me back to Kansas," said Dorothy.

"Then, if you don't mind, I'll go with you," said the Lion, "for my life is simply unbearable without a bit of courage."

So once more the little company set off upon the journey.

That night they were obliged to camp out under a

large tree in the forest, for there were no houses near. Dorothy and Toto ate the last of their bread, and now she did not know what they would do for breakfast. The Lion went away into the forest and found his own supper, and no one ever knew what it was, for he didn't mention it.

Meanwhile, during Dorothy's sleep, the Scarecrow found a tree full of nuts and filled Dorothy's basket with them, so that she would not be hungry for a long time.

When it was daylight the girl bathed her face in a little rippling brook and soon after they all started toward the Emerald City.

3

The Journey to the Great Oz

THEY FOUND the forest very thick, and it looked gloomy. They were silently wondering, each in his own mind, if ever they would come to the end of the woods and reach the bright sunlight again. They walked so fast that Dorothy became tired, and had to ride on the Lion's back. To their great joy the trees became thinner the further they advanced, and in the afternoon they suddenly came upon a broad river, flowing swiftly just before them. On the other side of the water they could see the road of yellow brick

running through a beautiful country, with green
meadows dotted with bright flowers and all the road
bordered with trees hanging full of delicious fruit.

"How shall we cross the river?" asked Dorothy.

"The Tin Woodman must build us a raft, so we can
float to the other side," said the Scarecrow.

So the Woodman took his axe and began to chop
down small trees to make a raft. After the Tin Woodman had cut many logs and fastened them together
with wooden pins, they were ready to start. Dorothy
sat down in the middle of the raft and held Toto in
her arms. The Scarecrow and the Tin Woodman had
long poles in their hands to push the raft through the
water.

They got along quite well at first, but when they

reached the middle of the river the swift current swept the raft down stream, farther and farther away from the road of yellow brick; and the water grew so deep that the long poles would not touch the bottom.

"This is bad," said the Tin Woodman, "for if we cannot get to the land we shall be carried into the country of the Wicked Witch of the West, and she will enchant us and make us her slaves."

"And then I should get no brains," said the Scarecrow.

"And I should get no courage," said the Cowardly Lion.

"And I should get no heart," said the Tin Woodman.

"And I should never get back to Kansas," said Dorothy.

Down the stream the raft floated. Then the Lion said, "Something must be done to save us. I think I can swim to the shore and pull the raft after me, if you will only hold fast to the tip of my tail."

So he sprang into the water and the Tin Woodman caught fast hold of his tail. The great Lion swam with all his might toward the shore, and at last they reached land.

When they all were rested, Dorothy picked up her basket and they started along the grassy bank, back to the road from which the river had carried them. They walked along listening to the singing of the bright-colored birds and looking at the lovely flowers which now became so thick that the ground was carpeted with them. There were big yellow and white and blue and purple blossoms, besides great clusters of scarlet poppies, which were so brilliant in color they almost dazzled Dorothy's eyes.

They came upon more and more of the big scarlet poppies, and fewer and fewer of the other flowers; and soon they found themselves in the midst of a great meadow of poppies. It is well known that when there are many of these flowers together their odor is so powerful that anyone who breathes it falls asleep, and if the sleeper is not carried away from the scent of the flowers he sleeps on and on forever. But Dorothy did not know this, nor could she get away from the bright red flowers that were everywhere about; so soon her eyes grew heavy and she felt she must sit down to rest and to sleep.

But the Tin Woodman would not let her do this.

"We must hurry and get back to the road of yellow brick before dark," he said; and the Scarecrow agreed with him. So they kept walking until Dorothy could stand no longer. Her eyes closed in spite of herself and she forgot where she was and fell among the poppies, fast asleep.

"What shall we do?" asked the Tin Woodman.

"If we leave her here she will die," said the Lion. "The smell of the flowers is killing us all. I myself can scarcely keep my eyes open, and the dog is asleep already."

The Scarecrow and the Tin Woodman, not being made of flesh, were not troubled by the scent of the flowers.

"Run fast," said the Scarecrow to the Lion, "and get out of this deadly flower-bed as soon as you can. We will bring the girl with us, but if you should fall asleep you are too big to be carried."

So the Lion roused himself and bounded foward as fast as he could go. In a moment he was out of sight.

"Let us make a chair with our hands and carry her," said the Scarecrow. So they picked up Toto and put the dog in Dorothy's lap, and then carried the sleeping girl between them through the flowers.

On and on they walked, and it seemed that the great carpet of deadly flowers that surrounded them would never end.

They carried the sleeping girl to a pretty spot beside the river, where the Lion was sleeping, far enough from the poppy field to prevent her breathing any more of the poison of the flowers, and they laid her gently on the soft grass and waited for the fresh breeze to waken her.

When Dorothy and the Lion woke up, they all started upon their journey, greatly enjoying the walk through the soft, fresh grass; and it was not long before they reached the road of yellow brick and turned again toward the Emerald City where the great Oz lived.

The road was smooth and well paved, now, and the country about was beautiful. Once more they could see houses built beside the road; but these were painted green. They passed by several of these houses during the afternoon, and sometimes people came to the doors and looked at them; but no one came near them nor spoke to them because of the great Lion. The people were all dressed in clothing of a lovely emerald green color and wore peaked hats like those of the Munchkins.

When they came to a good sized farm house, Dorothy walked boldly up to the door and knocked. A woman opened it just far enough to look out, and said, "What do you want, child, and why is that great Lion with you?"

"We wish to pass the night with you, if you will allow us," answered Dorothy; "and the Lion is my friend, and would not hurt you for the world."

"Well," said the woman, "if that is the case you may come in, and I will give you some supper and a place to sleep."

So they all entered the house, where there were, besides the woman, two children and a man. The man asked, "Where are you all going?"

"To the Emerald City," said Dorothy, "to see the Great Oz."

"Oh, indeed!" exclaimed the man. "I have never been permitted to see the Great Oz, nor do I know of any living person who has seen him. He sits day after day in the great throne room of his palace, and even those who wait upon him do not see him face to face."

"What is he like?" asked the girl.

"That is hard to tell," said the man. "You see, Oz is a great Wizard, and can take on any form he wishes. Some say he looks like a bird; and some say he looks like an elephant; and some say he looks like a cat. To others he appears as a beautiful fairy, or a brownie, or in any other form that pleases him. But who the real Oz is, when he is in his own form, no living person can tell."

"That is very strange," said Dorothy; "but we must try to see him, or we shall have made our journey for nothing."

The woman now called to them that supper was ready, so they gathered around the table and Dorothy ate some delicious porridge and a dish of scrambled eggs and a plate of nice white bread, and enjoyed her meal. The Lion ate some of the porridge, but did not care for it, saying it was made from oats and oats were food for horses, not for lions. The Scarecrow and the Tin Woodman ate nothing at all. Toto ate a little of everything, and was glad to get a good supper again.

The woman now gave Dorothy a bed to sleep in, and Toto lay down beside her, while the Lion guarded the door of her room so she might not be disturbed. The Scarecrow and the Tin Woodman stood up in a corner and kept quiet all night, although of course they could not sleep.

The next morning, as soon as the sun was up, they started on their way, and soon saw a beautiful green glow in the sky just before them.

"That must be the Emerald City," said Dorothy.

As they walked on, the green glow became brighter and brighter, and it seemed that at last they were nearing the end of their travels. Yet it was afternoon before they came to the great wall that surrounded the city.

At the end of the road of yellow brick, was a big gate, all studded with emeralds. There was a bell beside the gate, and Dorothy pushed the button and heard a silvery tinkle. Then the big gate swung slowly open, and they all passed through and found themselves in a high arched room.

Before them stood a little man about the same size as the Munchkins. He was clothed all in green, and even his skin was of a greenish tint. At his side was a large green box.

"What do you wish in the Emerald City?" he asked.

"We came to see the Great Oz," said Dorothy.

"It has been many years since anyone asked me to see Oz," he said. "He is powerful and terrible, and if you come on an idle or foolish errand to bother the wise reflections of the Great Wizard, he might be angry and destroy you all in an instant."

"But it is not a foolish errand, nor an idle one," replied the Scarecrow; "it is important."

"Since you demand to see the Great Oz I must take you to his palace. But first you must put on the spectacles," said the Guardian of the Gate. "If you did not wear spectacles the brightness and glory of the Emerald City would blind you. Even those who live in the City must wear spectacles night and day. They are all locked on, for Oz so ordered it when the City was first built, and I have the only key that will unlock them."

He opened a big box, and Dorothy saw that it was filled with spectacles of every size and shape. All of them had green glasses in them. The Guardian fitted spectacles for all of them, and all were locked fast with the key.

Then the Guardian of the Gate put on his own glasses and, taking a big golden key from a peg, he opened another gate, and they all followed him through the portal into the streets of the Emerald City.

4

The Emerald City and the Wizard

THE STREETS were lined with beautiful houses all built of green marble and studded everywhere with sparkling emeralds. They walked over a pavement of the same green marble. The window panes were of green glass; even the sky above the city had a green tint, and the rays of the sun were green.

There were many people, men, women and children, walking about, and they were all dressed in green clothes and had greenish skins. They looked at Dorothy and her company, and the children all ran away and hid behind their mothers when they saw the Lion; but no one spoke to them. Many shops stood in the street. Green candy and green popcorn were offered for sale, as well as green shoes, green hats and green clothes of all sorts. A man was selling green lemonade, and when the children bought it they paid for it with green pennies.

The Guardian of the Gate led them through the streets until they came to a big building, exactly in the middle of the City, which was the Palace of Oz, the Great Wizard. There was a soldier before the door, dressed in a green uniform and wearing a long green beard.

"Here are strangers," said the Guardian of the Gate, "and they demand to see the Great Oz."

"Step inside," said the soldier, "and I will carry your message to him."

They had to wait a long time before the soldier returned.

"Have you seen Oz?" asked Dorothy.

"Oh, no," said the soldier. "I have never seen him. But I spoke to him as he sat behind his screen, and gave him your message. He says he will grant you an audience; but each one of you must enter his presence alone, and he will admit but one each day. Therefore, as you must remain in the palace for several days, I will have you shown to rooms where you may rest in comfort after your journey."

The soldier now blew upon a green whistle, and at once a young girl, dressed in a pretty green silk gown, entered the room. She had lovely green hair and green eyes, and she bowed low before Dorothy as she said, "Follow me and I will show you your room."

So Dorothy said goodbye to all her friends except Toto, and taking the dog in her arms followed the green girl. The room at the front of the palace was the sweetest little room in the world, with a soft bed that had sheets of green silk and a green velvet bedspread. There was a tiny fountain in the middle of the room, that shot a spray of green perfume into the air. Beautiful green flowers stood in the windows, and there was a shelf with a row of little green books.

In a wardrobe were many green dresses, made of silk and satin and velvet; and all of them fitted Dorothy exactly.

"Make yourself at home," said the green girl, "and if you wish for anything ring the bell. Oz will send for you tomorrow morning."

She left Dorothy alone and went back to the others. These she also led to rooms, and each one of them found himself lodged in a very pleasant part of the palace.

The next morning, after breakfast, the green maiden came to fetch Dorothy, and she dressed her in one of the prettiest gowns that were in the wardrobe—made of green brocaded satin.

The green girl led Dorothy through the great hall to the Throne Room. When the bell rang, the green girl said to Dorothy, "That is the signal. You must go into the Throne Room alone."

She opened a little door and Dorothy walked

through and found herself in a wonderful place. It was a big, round room with a high arched roof, and the walls and ceiling and floor were covered with large emeralds.

What interested Dorothy most was the big throne of green marble that stood in the middle of the room. It was shaped like a chair and sparkled with gems, as did everything else. In the center of the chair was an enormous Head, without body to support it or any arms or legs whatever. There was no hair upon this head, but it had eyes and nose and mouth, and was bigger than the head of the biggest giant.

The eyes turned slowly and looked at her. Then the mouth moved, and Dorothy heard a voice say: "I am Oz, the Great and Terrible. Who are you, and why do you seek me?"

"I am Dorothy, the Small and Meek. I have come to you for help."

"Where did you get the silver shoes?"

"I got them from the Wicked Witch of the East, when my house fell on her and killed her," she replied.

"Where did you get that mark upon your forehead?"

"That is where the good Witch of the North kissed me when she bade me goodbye and sent me to you," said the girl.

The voice asked, "What do you wish me to do?"

"Send me back to Kansas, where my Aunt Em and Uncle Henry are," she answered.

The eyes winked three times, and then they turned

up to the ceiling and down to the floor and moved around so oddly that they seemed to see every part of the room. And at last they looked at Dorothy again.

"Why should I do this for you?" asked Oz.

"Because you are strong and I am weak; because you are a Great Wizard and I am only a helpless little girl."

"But you were strong enough to kill the Wicked Witch of the East," said Oz.

"That just happened," said Dorothy. "I could not help it."

"Well," said the Head, "I will give you my answer. You have no right to expect me to send you back to Kansas unless you do something for me in return. In this country everyone must pay for everything he gets. If you wish me to use my magic power to send you home again you must do something for me first."

"What must I do?"

"Kill the Wicked Witch of the West," answered Oz.

"But I cannot!" exclaimed Dorothy.

"You killed the Witch of the East and you wear the silver shoes, which bear a powerful charm. There is now but one Wicked Witch left in all this land, and when you can tell me she is dead I will send you back to Kansas—but not before."

The little girl began to weep. "I never killed anything, willingly," she sobbed; "and even if I wanted to, how could I kill the Wicked Witch? If you, who are Great and Terrible, cannot kill her yourself, how do you expect me to do it?"

"I do not know," said the Head; "but that is my answer, and until the Wicked Witch dies you will not see your Uncle and Aunt again."

Dorothy left the Throne Room and went back where the Lion and the Scarecrow and the Tin Woodman were waiting to hear what Oz had said to her.

"There is no hope for me," she said, "for Oz will not send me home until I have killed the Wicked Witch of the West; and that I can never do."

Her friends were sorry, but could do nothing to help her; so she went to her room and lay down and cried herself to sleep.

The next morning the soldier with the green whiskers came to the Scarecrow and said, "Come with me, for Oz has sent for you."

So the Scarecrow followed him and was admitted into the great Throne Room, where he saw, sitting in the emerald throne, a most lovely Lady. She was dressed in green silk and wore upon her flowing green locks a crown of jewels.

When the Scarecrow had bowed before this beautiful creature, she said, "I am Oz, the Great and Terrible. Who are you, and why do you seek me?"

The Scarecrow, who had expected to see the great Head Dorothy had told him of, was much astonished, but he answered, "I am only a Scarecrow, stuffed with straw. Therefore I have no brains, and I come to you praying that you will put brains in my head instead of straw, so that I may become as much a man as any other in your dominions."

"Why should I do this for you?" asked the Lady.

"Because you are wise and powerful, and no one else can help me," said the Scarecrow.

"I never grant favors without some return," said Oz; "but this much I will promise. If you will kill for me the Wicked Witch of the West I will bestow upon you a great many brains, and such good brains that you will be the wisest man in all the Land of Oz."

"I thought you asked Dorothy to kill the Witch," said the Scarecrow.

"So I did. I don't care who kills her. But until she is dead I will not grant your wish. Now go, and do not seek me again until you have earned the brains you desire."

The Scarecrow went back to his friends and told them what Oz had said.

On the next morning the soldier with the green whiskers came to the Tin Woodman and said, "Oz has sent for you. Follow me."

So the Tin Woodman followed him and came to the great Throne Room.

When the Woodman entered he saw neither the Head nor the Lady, for Oz had taken the shape of a most terrible Beast. It was nearly as big as an elephant, and the green throne seemed hardly strong enough to hold its weight. The Beast had a head like that of a rhinoceros, only there were five eyes in its face. There were five long arms growing out of its body and it also had five long, slim legs. Thick, woolly hair covered every part of it.

"I am Oz, the Great and Terrible," said the Beast, in a voice that was one great roar. "Who are you and why do you seek me?"

"I am a Woodman, and made of tin. Therefore I have no heart, and cannot love. I pray you to give me a heart that I may be as other men are."

"Why should I do this?"

"Because I ask it, and you alone can grant my request," said the Woodman.

"If you indeed desire a heart, you must earn it."

"How?" asked the Woodman.

"Help Dorothy to kill the Wicked Witch of the West," replied the Beast. "When the Witch is dead, come to me, and I will then give you the biggest and kindest and most loving heart in all the Land of Oz."

So the Tin Woodman was forced to return to his friends and tell them of the terrible Beast he had seen.

"If he is a beast when I go to see him," said the Lion, "I shall roar my loudest and so frighten him that he will grant all I ask. And if he is the lovely Lady, I shall pretend to spring upon her, and so compel her to do my bidding. And if he is the great Head, he will be at my mercy; for I will roll his head all about the

room until he promises to give us what we desire. So be of good cheer, my friends, for all will yet be well."

The next morning the soldier with the green whiskers led the Lion to the great Throne Room and bade· him enter the presence of Oz.

The Lion passed through the door, and saw, to his surprise, that before the throne was a Ball of Fire, so fierce and glowing he could scarcely bear to gaze upon it. His first thought was that Oz had by accident caught on fire and was burning up; but, when he tried to go nearer, the heat was so intense that it singed his whiskers, and he crept back to a spot nearer the door.

Then a low, quiet voice came from the Ball of Fire: "I am Oz, the Great and Terrible. Who are you, and why do you seek me?"

"I am a Cowardly Lion, afraid of everything. I come to you to beg that you give me courage, so that in reality I may become the King of Beasts, as men call me."

"Why should I give you courage?"

"Because of all Wizards you are the greatest, and alone have power to grant my request."

The voice said, "Bring me proof that the Wicked Witch is dead, and that moment I will give you courage. But so long as the Witch lives you must remain a coward."

It became so hot that the Lion turned tail and rushed from the room. He was glad to find his friends waiting for him, and told them of his terrible interview with the Wizard.

"What shall we do now?" asked Dorothy.

"There is only one thing we can do," said the Lion, "and that is to go to the yellow land of the West, seek out the Wicked Witch, and destroy her."

"But suppose we cannot?" said the girl.

"Then I shall never have courage," said the Lion.

"And I shall never have brains," added the Scarecrow.

"And I shall never have a heart," spoke the Tin Woodman.

"And I shall never see Aunt Em and Uncle Henry," said Dorothy. "I suppose we must try it; but I am sure I do not want to kill anybody, even to see Aunt Em again."

5

The Wicked Witch

IT WAS decided to start upon their journey the next morning, and the Woodman sharpened his axe on a green grindstone and had all his joints properly oiled. The Scarecrow stuffed himself with fresh straw and Dorothy put new paint on his eyes that he might see better. The green girl, who was very kind to them, filled Dorothy's basket with good things to eat, and fastened a little bell around Toto's neck with a green ribbon.

In the morning the Guardian of the Gate unlocked their spectacles to put them back in his box, and then he opened the gate for our friends.

"Which road leads to the Wicked Witch of the West?" asked Dorothy.

"There is no road," answered the Guardian of the Gate; "no one ever wishes to go that way, for she is wicked and fierce. But keep to the west, where the sun sets, and you cannot fail to find her."

They thanked him and bade him goodbye, and turned toward the west, walking over fields of soft grass dotted here and there with daisies and buttercups. Dorothy still wore the pretty silk dress she had put on in the palace, but now she found it was no longer green, but pure white. The ribbon around Toto's neck had also lost its green color and was as white as Dorothy's dress.

In the afternoon the sun shone hot in their faces, for there were no trees; so that before night Dorothy and Toto and the Lion were tired, and lay down upon the grass and fell asleep, with the Woodman and the Scarecrow keeping watch.

Now the Wicked Witch of the West had but one eye, yet that was as powerful as a telescope, and could see everywhere. So, as she sat in the door of her castle, she happened to look around and saw Dorothy lying asleep, with her friends all about her. They were a long distance off, but the Wicked Witch was angry to find them in her yellow country; she called a dozen of her slaves, who were the Winkies, and gave them sharp spears, telling them to go to the strangers and destroy them.

The Winkies were not a brave people; but they had to do as they were told; so they marched away until they came near to Dorothy. Then the Lion gave a great roar and sprang toward them, and the poor Winkies were so frightened that they ran back as fast as they could.

When they returned to the castle the Wicked Witch beat them well with a strap, and sent them back to their work, after which she sat down to think what she should do next.

There was, in her cupboard, a Golden Cap, with a circle of diamonds and rubies running round it. This cap had a charm. Whoever owned it could call three times upon the Winged Monkeys, who would obey any order they were given. But no person could command these strange creatures more than three times. Twice already the Wicked Witch had used the charm of the cap. Once was when she had made the Winkies her slaves, and set herself to rule over their country. The Winged Monkeys had helped her do this. The second time was when she had fought against the Great Oz himself, and driven him out of the land of the West. The Winged Monkeys had also helped her in doing this.

The Wicked Witch took the Golden Cap from her cupboard and placed it upon her head. Then she stood upon her left foot and said, "Ep-pe, pep-pe, kak-ke!"

Next she stood upon her right foot and said, "Hil-lo, hol-lo, hel-lo!"

After this she stood upon both feet and cried in a loud voice, "Ziz-zy, zuz-zy, zik!"

Now the charm began to work. There was a rushing of many wings; a great chattering and laughing. The Wicked Witch was soon surrounded by a crowd of monkeys, each with a pair of immense and powerful wings on his shoulders.

The biggest one, their leader, flew close to the Witch and said, "You have called us for the third and last time. What do you command?"

"Go to the strangers who are within my land and destroy them all except the Lion. Bring that beast to me, for I have a mind to harness him like a horse, and make him work."

"Your commands shall be obeyed," said the leader. And then, with a great deal of chattering and noise, the Winged Monkeys flew away to the place where Dorothy and her friends were walking.

Some of the Monkeys seized the Tin Woodman and carried him through the air until they were over sharp rocks. Here they dropped the poor Woodman, who fell a great distance to the rocks, where he lay so battered and dented that he could neither move nor groan.

Others of the Monkeys caught the Scarecrow, and with their long fingers pulled all of the straw out of his clothes and head. They made his hat and boots and clothes into a small bundle and threw it into the top branches of a tall tree.

The remaining Monkeys threw pieces of rope around the Lion and wound many coils about his body and head and legs, until he was unable to bite or scratch. Then they lifted him up and flew away with him to the Witch's castle.

But Dorothy they did not harm at all. She stood, with Toto in her arms, watching the sad fate of her comrades and thinking it would soon be her turn. The leader of the Winged Monkeys flew up to her, but

he saw the mark of the Good Witch's kiss upon her forehead and stopped short, motioning to the others not to touch her.

"We dare not harm this little girl," he said to them, "for she is protected by the Power of Good, and that is more powerful than the Power of Evil. All we can do is to carry her to the castle of the Wicked Witch and leave her there."

They lifted Dorothy in their arms and carried her through the air until they came to the yellow castle, where they set her down upon the front door step. Then the leader said to the Witch, "We have obeyed you as far as we were able. The little girl we dare not harm, nor the dog she carries. Your power over our band is now ended, and you will never see us again."

Then all the Winged Monkeys flew into the air and were soon out of sight.

The Wicked Witch was worried when she saw the mark on Dorothy's forehead, for she knew well that neither the Winged Monkeys nor she, herself, dare hurt the girl in any way. She looked down at Dorothy's feet, and seeing the Silver Shoes, began to tremble with fear, for she knew what a powerful charm belonged to them. But then she laughed to herself and thought, "I can still make the little girl my slave, for she does not know how to use her power." Then she said to Dorothy, "Come with me; and see that you mind everything I tell you, for if you do not I will make an end of you, as I did of the Tin Woodman and the Scarecrow."

The Witch brought her to the kitchen, where she bade Dorothy clean the pots and kettles and sweep the floor.

Then the Witch went to harness the Lion. But as she opened the gate the Lion gave a loud roar and bounded out at her. The Witch was afraid, and ran out and shut the gate. "If I cannot harness you," she said to the Lion, "I can starve you. You shall have nothing to eat until you do as I wish."

Every day she came to the gate and asked him, "Are you ready to be harnessed like a horse?"

And the Lion would answer, "No. If you come in this yard I will bite you."

The reason the Lion did not have to do as the Witch wished was that every night, while the woman was asleep, Dorothy carried him food. After he had eaten he would lie down on his bed of straw, and Dorothy would lie beside him and put her head on his soft, shaggy mane, while they talked of their troubles and tried to plan some way of escape.

The girl had to work hard during the day, and often the Witch threatened to beat her. But she did not dare to strike Dorothy, because of the mark upon her forehead. The child did not know this, and was full of fear for herself. Once the Witch struck Toto a blow with her umbrella and the brave little dog flew at her and bit her leg, in return. The Witch did not bleed where she was bitten, for she was so wicked that the blood in her had dried up many years before.

The Wicked Witch had a great longing to have for

her own the Silver Shoes which the girl always wore. The child was so proud of her pretty shoes that she never took them off except at night and when she took her bath. The Witch was too much afraid of the dark to dare go in Dorothy's room at night to take the shoes, and her dread of water was greater than her fear of the dark, so she never came near when Dorothy was bathing. Indeed, the old Witch never touched water, nor ever let water touch her in any way.

But the wicked creature was very cunning, and she thought of a trick that would give her what she wanted. She placed an invisible bar of iron in the middle of the kitchen floor, and when Dorothy walked across the floor she stumbled over the bar, not being able to see it, and fell at full length. In her fall one of her Silver Shoes came off, and before she could reach it the Witch had snatched it away and put it on her own skinny foot.

The little girl, seeing she had lost one of her pretty shoes, grew angry, and said to the Witch, "Give me back my shoe!"

"I will not," retorted the Witch, "for it is now my shoe, and not yours."

"You are a wicked creature!" cried Dorothy. "You have no right to take my shoe from me."

"I shall keep it just the same," said the Witch, laughing at her, "and someday I shall get the other one from you, too."

This made Dorothy so very angry that she picked up the bucket of water that stood near and dashed it over the Witch, wetting her from head to foot.

The wicked woman gave a loud cry of fear; and then, as Dorothy looked at her, the Witch began to shrink and fall away.

"I'm very sorry, indeed," said Dorothy, who was frightened to see the Witch melting away like brown sugar before her eyes.

"Didn't you know water would be the end of me?" asked the Witch.

"Of course not," said Dorothy.

"Well, in a few minutes I shall be all melted, and

you will have the castle to yourself. I have been wicked in my day, but I never thought a little girl like you would ever be able to melt me and end my wicked deeds. Look out—here I go!"

With these words the Witch fell down in a brown, melted, shapeless mass and began to spread over the clean boards of the kitchen floor. Seeing that she had really melted away to nothing, Dorothy drew another bucket of water and threw it over the mess. She then swept it all out the door. After picking out the silver shoe, which was all that was left of the old woman, she cleaned and dried it with a cloth, and put it on her foot again. Then she ran out to the court-yard to tell the Lion that the Wicked Witch of the West had come to an end, and that they were no longer prisoners in a strange land.

From the court-yard they went in together to the castle, where Dorothy called the Winkies together and told them that they were no longer slaves.

There was great rejoicing among the Winkies, for they had been made to work hard during many years for the Wicked Witch.

The Lion and Dorothy asked the Winkies if they would help to rescue their friends, the Scarecrow and the Tin Woodman, and the Winkies said that they would be delighted to do all in their power for Dorothy, who had set them free.

They travelled that day and part of the next until they came to the rocks where the Tin Woodman lay, all battered and bent.

The Winkies lifted him and carried him back to the castle.

"Are any of your people tinsmiths?" asked Dorothy.

"Oh, yes," a Winkie told her.

"Then bring them to me," she said. And when the tinsmiths came, she asked, "Can you straighten out those dents in the Tin Woodman, and bend him back into shape again, and solder him together where he is broken?"

The tinsmiths looked the Woodman over and answered that they thought they could mend him so he would be as good as ever. So they set to work for three days and four nights, hammering and pounding at the legs and body and head of the Tin Woodman, until at last he was straightened out into his old form, and his joints worked as well as ever.

When he walked into Dorothy's room and thanked her for rescuing him, he was so pleased that he wept tears of joy, and Dorothy had to wipe every tear from his face with her apron, so his joints would not be rusted.

"If we only had the Scarecrow with us again," said the Tin Woodman, "I should be quite happy."

Dorothy called the Winkies to help her, and they walked all that day and part of the next until they came to the tall tree in the branches of which the Winged Monkeys had tossed the Scarecrow's clothes.

It was a very tall tree, and the trunk was so smooth that no one could climb it. The Tin Woodman started chopping the tree, and when the tree fell over with a crash, the Scarecrow's clothes fell out of the branches.

Dorothy picked them up and had the Winkies carry them back to the castle, where they were stuffed with nice, clean straw; and, behold! here was the Scarecrow, as good as ever, thanking them over and over again for saving him.

6

The Wizard's Secret

NOW THEY were reunited, Dorothy and her friends spent a few happy days at the yellow castle, where they found everything they needed to make them comfortable. But one day the girl thought of Aunt Em and said, "We must go back to Oz, and claim his promise."

"Yes," said the Woodman, "at last I shall get my heart."

"And I shall get my brains," added the Scarecrow.

"And I shall get my courage," said the Lion.

"And I shall get back to Kansas," cried Dorothy.

The next day they called the Winkies together and bade them goodbye. The Winkies were sorry to have them go, and they had grown so fond of the Tin Woodman that they begged him to stay and rule over them and the Yellow Land of the West.

When Dorothy went to the Witch's cupboard to fill her basket with food for the journey, she saw the Golden Cap. She tried it on and found that it fitted her exactly. She did not know anything about the charm of the Golden Cap, but she saw that it was pretty, so she wore it and carried her sunbonnet in the basket.

Then, they all started for the Emerald City; and the Winkies gave them three cheers and many good wishes.

You will remember there was no road between the castle of the Wicked Witch and the Emerald City. It was much harder to find their way back through the big fields of buttercups and yellow daisies than it was being carried by Winged Monkeys. They got lost and spent the first night sleeping among the sweet smelling yellow flowers.

The next morning they started on, as if they were quite sure which way they were going. "If we walk far enough," said Dorothy, "we shall sometime come to some place, I am sure."

But day by day passed away, and they still saw nothing before them but yellow fields.

Finally, the Queen of the Field Mice stopped by them, and asked, "What can I do for you, friends?"

"We have lost our way," said Dorothy. "Can you tell us where the Emerald City is?"

"Certainly," said the Queen. Then she noticed Dorothy's Golden Cap, and said, "Why don't you use the charm of the cap, and call the Winged Monkeys to you? They will carry you to the city of Oz in less than an hour."

"I didn't know there was a charm," said Dorothy. "What is it?"

"It is written inside the Golden Cap," replied the Queen of the Mice. "Goodbye!"

Dorothy looked inside the Golden Cap and saw some words written upon the lining. She read the directions carefully and put the cap upon her head.

"Ep-pe, pep-pe, kak-ke!" she said, standing on her left foot.

"What did you say?" asked the Scarecrow.

"Hil-lo, hol-lo, hel-lo!" Dorothy went on, standing this time on her right foot.

"Hello!" said the Tin Woodman.

"Ziz-zy, zuz-zy, zik!" said Dorothy, who was now standing on both feet. This ended the saying of the charm, and they heard a great chattering and flapping of wings, as the band of Winged Monkeys flew up to them.

The leader bowed low before Dorothy, and asked, "What is your command?"

"We wish to go to the Emerald City," said the child, "and we have lost our way."

"We will carry you," said the Winged Monkey, and no sooner had he spoken than two of the Monkeys caught Dorothy in their arms and flew away with her. Others took the Scarecrow and the Woodman and the Lion, and one little Monkey seized Toto and flew after them, although the dog tried hard to bite him.

They all rode through the air quite cheerfully, and had a fine time looking at the pretty gardens and woods far below them.

Dorothy looked down and saw the green shining walls of the Emerald City below them. The Winged Monkeys set the travellers down carefully before the gate of the city, the leader bowed low to Dorothy, and then flew swiftly away, followed by all his band.

"That was a good ride," said the little girl.

"Yes, and a quick way out of our troubles," replied the Lion. "How lucky it was you brought away that wonderful cap!"

The travellers walked up to the great gate of the Emerald City and rang the bell. "What! are you back again?" asked the Guardian of the Gate. "I thought you had gone to visit the Wicked Witch of the West."

"We did visit her," said the Scarecrow.

"And she let you go again?" asked the man.

"She could not help it, for she is melted," said the Scarecrow.

"Melted! Well, that is good news, indeed," said the man. "Who melted her?"

"It was Dorothy," said the Lion.

"Good gracious," exclaimed the man.

Then he led them into his little room and locked the spectacles from the box on all their eyes, just as he had done before. When the people heard from the Guardian of the Gate that they had melted the Wicked Witch of the West, they all gathered around the travellers and followed them in a great crowd to the Palace of Oz.

The soldier with the green whiskers was still on guard before the door, but he let them in immediately and they were again met by the beautiful green girl, who showed each of them to their old rooms, so they might rest until the Great Oz was ready to receive them.

They thought the Great Wizard would send for them at once, but he did not. They had no word from him the next day, nor the next, nor the next. The Scarecrow asked the green girl to take another message to Oz, saying if he did not let them in to see him they would call the Winged Monkeys to help them. When the Wizard was given this message he was so frightened that he sent word for them to come to the Throne Room at four minutes after nine o'clock the next morning.

At nine o'clock the next morning the green whiskered soldier came to them, and four minutes later they all went into the Throne Room of the Great Oz.

They kept close to the door and closer to one another, for the stillness of the empty room was more dreadful than any of the forms they had seen Oz take.

Soon they heard a voice, seeming to come from somewhere near the top of the great dome, and it said, "I am Oz, the Great and Terrible. Why do you seek me?"

Dorothy asked, "Where are you?"

"I am everywhere," answered the voice, "but to the eyes of common mortals I am invisible."

"We have come to claim our promise, O Oz."

"What promise?" asked Oz.

"You promised to send me back to Kansas when the Wicked Witch was destroyed," said the girl.

"And you promised to give me brains," said the Scarecrow.

"And you promised to give me a heart," said the Tin Woodman.

"And you promised to give me courage," said the Cowardly Lion.

"Is the Wicked Witch really destroyed?" asked the voice.

"Yes," Dorothy answered, "I melted her with a bucket of water."

"Dear me," said the voice, "how sudden! Well, come to me tomorrow, for I must have time to think it over."

"We shan't wait a day longer," said the Scarecrow.

The Lion thought it might be as well to frighten the Wizard, so he gave a large roar, which was so fierce that Toto jumped away in alarm and tipped over the screen that stood in the corner. As it fell with a crash they saw, standing in just the spot the screen had hidden, a little old man, with a bald head and a wrinkled face, who seemed to be as surprised as they were. The Tin Woodman, raising his axe, rushed toward the little man and cried out, "Who are you?"

"I am Oz, the Great and Terrible," said the little man, in a trembling voice.

"I thought Oz was a great Head," said Dorothy.

"And I thought Oz was a lovely Lady," said the Scarecrow.

"And I thought Oz was a terrible Beast," said the Tin Woodman.

"And I thought Oz was a Ball of Fire," said the Lion.

"No; you are all wrong," said the little man. "I have been making believe."

"Making believe!" cried Dorothy. "Are you not a great Wizard?"

"Not a bit of it, my dear; I'm just a common man."

"You're more than that," said the Scarecrow, "you're a humbug."

"Doesn't anyone else know you're a humbug?" asked Dorothy.

"No one knows it but you four—and myself," replied Oz. "I have fooled everyone so long that I thought I should never be found out."

"But, I don't understand," said Dorothy. "How was it that you appeared to me as a great Head?"

"That was one of my tricks," answered Oz. He led the way to a small chamber in the rear of the Throne Room, and they all followed him. In one corner lay the Great Head, made out of paper, with a carefully painted face.

"This I hung from the ceiling by a wire," said Oz.

"But how about the voice?" Dorothy asked.

"Oh, I am a ventriloquist," said the little man, "and

I can throw the sound of my voice wherever I wish. Here are the other things I used to deceive you." He showed the Scarecrow the dress and mask he had worn when he seemed to be the lovely Lady; and the Tin Woodman saw that his Terrible Beast was nothing but a lot of skins, sewn together. As for the Ball of Fire, the false Wizard had hung that also from the ceiling. It was really a ball of cotton, but when oil was poured upon it the ball burned fiercely.

"Really," said the Scarecrow, "you ought to be ashamed of yourself for being such a humbug."

"I am," answered the man. "Sit down, please, and I will tell you my story."

They sat down and listened.

"I was born in Omaha—"

"Why, that isn't very far from Kansas," cried Dorothy.

"No; but it's far from here," he said. "When I grew up I became a ventriloquist. I can imitate any kind of a bird or beast. After a time, I tired of that, and became a balloonist for the circus. Well, one day I went up in a balloon and the ropes got twisted, so that I couldn't come down again. It went way up above the clouds and a current of air struck it and carried it many, many miles away. On the morning of the second day I awoke and found the balloon floating over a strange and beautiful country. It came down gradually, and I found myself in the midst of a strange people, who, seeing me come from the clouds, thought I was a great Wizard. They were afraid of me, and promised to do anything I wished them to.

"I ordered them to build this City, and my palace. Then I thought, as the country was so green and beautiful, I would call it the Emerald City, and to make the name fit better I put green spectacles on all the people, so that everything they saw was green."

"But isn't everything here green?" asked Dorothy.

"No more than in any other city," replied Oz. "But my people have worn green glasses on their eyes so long that most of them think it really is an Emerald City. I have been good to the people, and they like me; but ever since this palace was built I have not seen any of them.

"One of my greatest fears was the Witches, for while I had no magical powers at all I soon found out that the Witches were really able to do wonderful things. As it was, I lived in deadly fear of the Wicked Witches for many years; so you can imagine how pleased I was when I heard your house had fallen on the Wicked Witch of the East. When you came to me I was willing to promise anything if you would only do away with the other Witch; but, now that you have melted her, I am ashamed to say that I cannot keep my promises."

"I think you are a very bad man," said Dorothy.

"Oh, no, my dear; I'm really a very good man; but I'm a very bad Wizard, I must admit."

"Can't you give me brains?" asked the Scarecrow.

"You don't need them," said Oz. "You are learning something every day. A baby has brains, but it doesn't know much. Experience is the only thing that brings

knowledge, and the longer you are on earth the more experience you are sure to get."

"That may all be true," said the Scarecrow, "but I shall be very unhappy unless you give me brains."

"Well," said the Wizard, "if you come to me tomorrow morning, I will stuff your head with brains. I cannot tell you how to use them, however; you must find that out for yourself."

"How about my courage?" asked the Lion.

"You have plenty of courage," answered Oz. "All you need is confidence in yourself. There is no living thing that is not afraid when it faces danger. True courage is in facing danger when you are afraid, and that kind of courage you have in plenty."

"I shall be very unhappy unless you give me the sort of courage that makes one forget he is afraid," said the Lion.

"Very well; I will give you that sort of courage tomorrow."

"How about my heart?" asked the Tin Woodman.

"Having a heart makes most people unhappy. You are in luck not to have a heart."

"I will bear all unhappiness if you will give me a heart."

"Very well," said Oz. "Come to me tomorrow and you shall have a heart."

"And now," said Dorothy, "how am I to get back to Kansas?"

"We shall have to think about that," replied the little man. "I'll try to find a way to carry you over the desert. There is only one thing I ask in return for my help to you all. You must keep my secret and tell no one I am a humbug."

They agreed to say nothing, and went back to their rooms.

7

The Wizard's Gifts and Departure

IN THE morning the Scarecrow was the first to go to the Wizard in the Throne Room.

"I have come for my brains," said the Scarecrow.

"Oh, yes; sit down in that chair, please," replied Oz. "You must excuse me for taking your head off, but I shall have to do it in order to put your brains in their proper place."

"That's all right," said the Scarecrow. "You are quite welcome to take my head off, as long as it will be a better one when you put it on again."

So the Wizard unfastened the head and emptied out the straw. Then he entered the back room and took up a measure of bran, which he mixed with a great many pins and needles. Having shaken them together thoroughly, he filled the top of the Scarecrow's head with the mixture and stuffed the rest of the space with straw, to hold it in place. When he had fastened the Scarecrow's head on his body he said to him, "Hereafter you will be a great man, for I have given you a lot of bran-new brains."

The Scarecrow was pleased and proud, and having thanked Oz he went back to his friends.

"How do you feel?" asked Dorothy.

"I feel wise, indeed," he answered.

"Why are those pins and needles sticking out of your head?" asked the Tin Woodman.

"That is proof that he is sharp," remarked the Lion.

The Woodman now went to the Throne Room and said to Oz, "I have come for my heart."

"Very well," answered the little man. "But I shall have to cut a hole in your breast, so I can put your heart in the right place. I hope it won't hurt you."

"Oh, no," answered the Woodman. "I shall not feel it at all."

Oz took out a pretty heart made entirely of silk and stuffed with sawdust.

"Is it a kind heart?" asked the Tin Woodman.

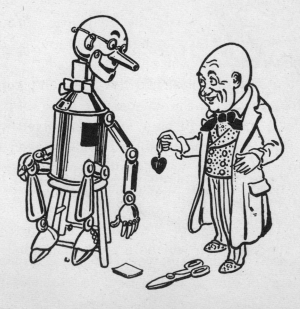

"Oh, very!" said Oz. He put the heart in the Wood-man's breast and then replaced the square of tin, soldering it neatly together.

"I am very grateful to you, and shall never forget your kindness," said the Tin Woodman.

Then he went back to his friends, who wished him every joy on account of his good fortune.

The Lion now walked to the Throne Room and knocked at the door. "I have come for my courage."

"Very well," answered Oz; "I will get it for you."

Oz poured the contents of a square green bottle into a green-gold dish. Placing this before the Cow-ardly Lion, the Wizard said, "Drink."

"What is it?"

"If it were inside you it would be courage," said Oz. "Courage is always inside one; so that this really cannot be called courage until you have swallowed it."

The Lion drank till it was empty.

"How do you feel now?" asked Oz.

"Full of courage," said the Lion, who went back to his friends to tell them of his good fortune.

Oz, left to himself, said, "How can I help being a humbug when all these people make me do things that everybody knows can't be done? It was easy to make the Scarecrow and the Lion and the Tin Woodman happy, because they imagined I could do anything. But it will take more than imagination to carry Dorothy back to Kansas."

For three days Dorothy heard nothing from Oz. On the fourth day, Oz sent for her, and when she entered the Throne Room, he said, "Sit down, my dear; I think I have found a way to get out of this country."

"How can I cross the desert?" she asked.

"You see, when I came to this country it was in a balloon. You also came through the air, being carried by a cyclone. Now, it is quite beyond my powers to make a cyclone; but I've been thinking the matter over, and I believe I can make a balloon. A balloon is made of silk, which is coated with glue to keep the gas in it. In this country there is no gas to fill the balloon, but there is another way to make it float, which is to fill it with hot air."

"Are you going with me?" asked the girl.

"Yes, of course," said Oz. "I am tired of being such a humbug. If I should go out of this palace my people would soon discover that I am not a Wizard, and then they would be vexed with me for having deceived them. I'd much rather go back to Kansas with you and be in a circus again. Now, if you will help me sew the silk together, we will begin to work on our balloon."

So Dorothy took a needle and thread, and as fast as Oz cut the strips of silk into proper shape the girl sewed them neatly together. It took three days to sew all the strips together, but when it was finished they had a big bag of green silk more than twenty feet long.

Oz sent the soldier with the green whiskers for a big clothes basket, which he fastened with many ropes to the bottom of the balloon.

When it was all ready, Oz sent word to his people that he was going to make a visit to a great brother Wizard who lived in the clouds.

The balloon was carried out in front of the palace, and the people gazed upon it with much curiosity. Oz held the bottom of the balloon over a fire so that hot air that arose from it would be caught in the silken bag. The balloon swelled out and rose into the air, until finally the basket just touched the ground.

Then Oz got into the basket and said to all the people: "While I am gone the Scarecrow will rule over you. I command you to obey him as you would me."

The balloon was by this time tugging hard at the rope that held it to the ground. "Come, Dorothy!" cried the Wizard; "hurry up, or the balloon will fly away!"

"I can't find Toto anywhere," replied Dorothy. Toto had run into the crowd to bark at a kitten, and Dorothy at last found him. She picked him up and ran toward the balloon.

She was within a few steps of it, and Oz was holding out his hands to help her into the basket, when, crack! went the ropes, and the balloon rose into the air without her.

"Come back!" she screamed; "I want to go, too!"

"I can't come back, my dear," called Oz from the basket. "Goodbye!"

And that was the last any of them ever saw of Oz, the Wonderful Wizard, though he may have reached Omaha safely, and be there now, for all we know.

"If Dorothy would only be contented to live in the Emerald City," said the Scarecrow, "we might all be happy together."

"But I don't want to live here," cried Dorothy. "I want to go to Kansas, and live with Aunt Em and Uncle Henry."

The Scarecrow decided to think, and he thought so hard that the pins and needles began to stick out of his brains. Finally he said: "Why not call the Winged Monkeys, and ask them to carry you over the desert?"

"I never thought of that!" said Dorothy. "I'll go at once for the Golden Cap."

When she brought it into the Throne Room she spoke the magic words, and soon the band of Winged Monkeys flew in through an open window and stood beside her.

"This is the second time you have called us," said the Monkey King. "What do you wish?"

"I want you to fly with me to Kansas."

"That cannot be done," said the Monkey King. "We cannot leave this country. We cannot cross the desert. Goodbye." With a bow the Monkey King spread his wings and flew away.

"Is there no one who can help me?" Dorothy asked their friend the green whiskered soldier.

"Glinda might," he replied. "She is the Witch of the South. She is the most powerful of all the Witches, and rules over the Quadlings. She is kind to everyone. I have heard that Glinda is a beautiful woman, who knows how to keep young in spite of the many years she has lived. The road is straight to the South, but it is said to be full of dangers to travellers."

The Scarecrow said, "It seems, in spite of dangers, that the best thing Dorothy can do is travel to the Land of the South and ask Glinda to help her."

"I shall go with Dorothy," declared the Lion, "for I

long for the woods and the country again. Besides, Dorothy will need someone to protect her."

"That is true," agreed the Woodman. "My axe may be of service to her; so I, also, will go with her to the Land of the South."

"I am going, also," said the Scarecrow. "If it wasn't for Dorothy I should never have had brains. I shall never leave her until she starts back to Kansas for good and all."

8

Glinda Aids Dorothy

THE NEXT morning the sun shone brightly on our friends as they turned their faces toward the Land of the South. The first day's journey was through the green fields and bright flowers that stretched about the Emerald City on every side. They slept that night on the grass, with nothing but the stars above them; and they rested very well indeed.

In the morning they travelled on until they came to a thick wood. There was no way of going around it, so they looked for the place where it would be easiest to get into the forest.

The Scarecrow, who was in the lead, discovered a big tree with wide spreading branches that had room for the party to pass underneath. Just as he came under the first branches they bent down and twined around him, and the next minute he was raised from the ground and flung headlong among his fellow travellers.

The Scarecrow walked up to another tree, but its branches immediately seized him and tossed him back again.

"This is strange," exclaimed Dorothy; "what shall we do?"

"I believe I will try it myself," said the Woodman, and shouldering his axe marched up to the first tree that had handled the Scarecrow so roughly. When a big branch bent down to seize him the Woodman chopped at it and cut it in two. At once the tree began shaking all its branches as if in pain, and the Tin Woodman passed safely under it.

"Come on!" he shouted to the others; "be quick!"

The other trees of the forest did nothing to keep them back, so they made up their minds that only the first row of trees could bend down their branches, and that probably these were the policemen of the

forest, and had been given this wonderful power to keep strangers out of it.

At the further edge of the wood, however, they found before them a high wall, which seemed to be made of white china. It was smooth, like the surface of a dish, and higher than their heads.

"I will make a ladder," said the Tin Woodman, "for we certainly must climb over the wall."

When they had all climbed the ladder and were sitting in a row on the top of the wall they looked down and saw a strange sight.

Before them was a great stretch of country having a floor as smooth and shining and white as the bottom of a big platter. Scattered around were many houses made entirely of china and painted in the brightest colors. These houses were quite small, the biggest of them reaching only as high as Dorothy's waist. There were also pretty little barns, with china fences around them, and many cows and sheep and horses and pigs and chickens, all made of china, were standing about in groups.

But the strangest of all were the people who lived in this odd country. There were milkmaids and shepherdesses and princesses and shepherds and princes and clowns. These people were all made of china, and were so small that the tallest of them was no higher than Dorothy's knee.

Dorothy and her friends walked carefully through the china country. The little animals and all the people scampered out of their way, fearing the strangers would break them, and after an hour or so the travellers reached the other side of the country and came to another china wall.

It was not as high as the first, however, and by standing upon the Lion's back they all managed to scramble to the top. Then the Lion jumped on the wall and followed them.

After climbing down from the wall, they found themselves in a disagreeable country, full of bogs and marshes. Then they entered another forest, where the trees were bigger and older than any they had ever seen.

"This forest is perfectly delightful," declared the Lion.

"It seems gloomy," said the Scarecrow.

They kept on until they came to an opening in the wood, in which were gathered hundreds of beasts of every variety. There were tigers and elephants and bears and wolves and foxes, and for a moment Dorothy was afraid. But the Lion explained that the animals were holding a meeting.

The biggest of the tigers came up to the Lion and bowed, saying, "Welcome, O King of Beasts! You have come in good time to fight our enemy and bring peace to all the animals of the forest once more. We are all threatened by an enemy which has lately come into this forest. It is a most tremendous monster, like a great spider, with a body as big as an elephant and legs as long as a tree trunk. It has eight of these long legs, and as the monster crawls through the forest he

seizes an animal with a leg and drags it to his mouth, where he eats it as a spider does a fly."

"If I put an end to your enemy will you bow down to me and obey me as King of the Forest?" asked the Lion.

"We will do that gladly," said the tiger; and all the other beasts roared, "We will!"

The Lion bade his friends goodbye and marched away to do battle with the enemy.

The great spider was lying asleep when the Lion found him. It had a great mouth, with a row of sharp teeth a foot long; but its head was joined to the pudgy body by a neck as slender as a wasp's waist. The Lion gave a great spring and landed directly upon the monster's back. Then, with one blow of his heavy paw, he knocked the spider's head from his body. He watched it until the long legs stopped wiggling, when he knew it was quite dead.

The Lion went back to the opening where the beasts were waiting for him and said, "You need fear your enemy no longer."

Then the beasts bowed down to the Lion as their King, and he promised to come back and rule over them as soon as Dorothy was safely on her way to Kansas.

The travellers passed through the rest of the forest in safety, and when they came out from its gloom saw before them a steep hill, covered from top to bottom with great pieces of rock. They had nearly reached the first rock when a head showed itself over the rock and said, "Keep back! This hill belongs to us, and we don't allow anyone to cross it."

There stepped from behind the rock the strangest man they had ever seen.

He was quite short and stout and had a big head, which was flat at the top and supported by a thick neck full of wrinkles. But he had no arms at all.

The Scarecrow said, "I'm sorry not to do as you wish, but we must pass over your hill whether you like it or not."

As quick as lightning the man's head shot forward and his neck stretched out until the top of the head, where it was flat, struck the Scarecrow in the middle and sent him tumbling over. A chorus of laughter came from the other rocks, and Dorothy saw hun-

dreds of the armless Hammer-Heads upon the hill-
side, one behind every rock.

"What can we do?" Dorothy asked her friends.

"Call the Winged Monkeys," suggested the Tin
Woodman.

"Very well," she said, and putting on the Golden
Cap she uttered the magic words. The Monkeys were
as prompt as ever.

"What are your commands?" asked the King of the
Monkeys.

"Carry us over the hill to the country of the Quadlings," said the girl.

"It shall be done," said the King, and at once the
Winged Monkeys caught the four travellers and Toto
up in their arms and flew away with them, carrying
them over the hill and down into the beautiful country
of the Quadlings.

"This is the last time you can summon us," said
the Monkey King to Dorothy; "so goodbye and good
luck."

"Goodbye and thank you very much," said Dorothy.

The country of the Quadlings seemed rich and
happy. The fences and bridges were all painted bright
red, just as they had been painted yellow in the
country of the Winkies and blue in the country of the
Munchkins.

They walked by fields and across the pretty bridges
until they saw before them a very beautiful castle.
Before the gates were three young girls, dressed in
handsome red uniforms trimmed with gold braid; and

as Dorothy approached, one of them said to her, "Why have you come to the South Country?"

"To see the Good Witch who rules here," she answered.

"Let me have your name and I will ask Glinda if she will receive you," said the soldier girl.

After a few moments she came back to say that Dorothy and the others were to be admitted at once.

They followed the soldier girl into a big room where the Witch Glinda sat upon a throne of rubies.

She was both beautiful and young to their eyes. Her hair was a rich red and fell in flowing ringlets over her shoulders. Her dress was pure white; but her eyes were blue.

"What can I do for you, my child?" she asked Dorothy.

Dorothy told the Witch all her story; how the cyclone had brought her to the Land of Oz, how she had found her companions, and of the wonderful adventures they had met with.

"My greatest wish now," she added, "is to get back to Kansas, for Aunt Em will surely think something dreadful has happened to me."

Glinda leaned forward and kissed the sweet face of the little girl. "Bless your dear heart," she said, "I am sure I can tell you of a way to get back to Kansas. But, if I do, you must give me the Golden Cap."

"Willingly!" exclaimed Dorothy, and gave her the cap.

The Witch turned and said to the Scarecrow, "What will you do when Dorothy has left us?"

"I will return to the Emerald City," he replied, "for Oz has made me its ruler and the people like me. The only thing that worries me is how to cross the hill of the Hammer-Heads."

"By means of the Golden Cap I shall command the Winged Monkeys to carry you to the gates of the Emerald City," said Glinda. Turning to the Tin Wood-man, she asked, "What will become of you when Dorothy leaves this country?"

"The Winkies were very kind to me, and wanted me to rule over them after the Wicked Witch died. I am fond of the Winkies, and if I could get back again to the country of the West I should like nothing better than to rule over them forever."

"My second command to the Winged Monkeys," said Glinda, "will be that they carry you safely to the

land of the Winkies." Then the Witch looked at the big, shaggy Lion and asked, "When Dorothy has returned to her own home, what will become of you?"

"Over the hill of the Hammer-Heads," he answered, "lies an old forest, and all the beasts that live there have made me their King. If I could only get back to this forest I would pass my life very happily."

"My third command to the Winged Monkeys," said Glinda, "shall be to carry you to your forest. Then, having used up the powers of the Golden Cap, I shall give it to the King of the Monkeys, and he and his band may thereafter be free forever."

And now to Dorothy, Glinda said, "Your Silver Shoes will carry you over the desert. If you had known their power you could have gone back to your Aunt Em the very first day you came to this country."

"But then I should not have had my wonderful brains!" cried the Scarecrow. "I might have passed my whole life in the farmer's cornfield."

"And I should not have had my lovely heart!" said the Tin Woodman. "I might have stood and rusted in the forest till the end of the world."

"And I should have lived a coward forever," declared the Lion, "and no beast would have had a good word to say to me."

"This is all true," said Dorothy, "and I am glad I was of use to these good friends. But now that each of them has had what he most desired, and each is happy in having a kingdom to rule, I think I should like to go back to Kansas."

"The Silver Shoes," said the Good Witch, "have wonderful powers. And one of them is that they can carry you to any place in the world in three steps, and each step will be made in the wink of an eye. All you have to do is knock the heels together three times and command the shoes to carry you wherever you wish to go."

Dorothy threw her arms around the Lion's neck and kissed him. Then she kissed the Tin Woodman, and hugged the soft, stuffed body of the Scarecrow in her arms instead of kissing his painted face, and found she was crying herself at this sorrowful parting from her loving friends.

Glinda the Good stepped down from her ruby throne to give the little girl a goodbye kiss, and

Dorothy thanked her for all the kindness she had shown to her friends and herself.

Dorothy now took Toto up in her arms, and having said one last goodbye she clapped the heels of her shoes together three times, saying, "Take me home to Aunt Em!"

Instantly she was whirling through the air, so swiftly that all she could see or feel was the wind whistling past her ears.

The Silver Shoes took but three steps, and then she stopped so suddenly that she rolled over upon the grass several times before she knew where she was. "Good gracious!" she cried.

She was sitting on the broad Kansas prairie, and just before her was the new farmhouse Uncle Henry built after the cyclone had carried away the old one. Uncle Henry was milking the cows in the barnyard, and Toto had jumped out of her arms and was running toward the barn, barking joyously.

Dorothy stood up and found she was in her stocking-feet. The Silver Shoes had fallen off in her flight through the air, and were lost forever in the desert.

Aunt Em had just come out of the house to water the cabbages when she looked up and saw Dorothy running toward her.

"My darling child!" she cried, folding the little girl in her arms and covering her face with kisses; "where in the world did you come from?"

"From the Land of Oz," said Dorothy. "And here is Toto, too. And oh, Aunt Em! I'm so glad to be at home again!"